Here we are again at
number 3 Tree Street.
Look, those chimps are up early.
They are swinging down on the rope.

They're getting on their bikes.
I wonder where they are going?
I hope they're not up to any mischief.

2

They're going past Mrs Snitchnose's house.
They're not doing any mischief there.
I wonder where they are going?

Ah, they're going to
Farmer Gibbon's farm.
They can't get up to any mischief there.

4

Oh dear, the animals look sad.
What a moo from Sunflower!
How now, brown cow?
What's the matter?

Oh dear, the goat does not want to play.
What is the matter?

6

Here comes Farmer Gibbon.
There has been no rain for weeks.
There is no grass for the animals to eat.

"We have plenty of grass," says Bangers.
"My Dad's always complaining about
having to cut the grass."

8

"We'll take them home."
Sunflower and the goat are tied to
the back of the bikes.
Off they go.

There they are by Mrs Snitchnose's house.
Oh dear, the goat is eating her hedge.
And Sunflower is eating her lettuces.

That's made them thirsty.
Don't drink all the pond, Sunflower!

There they are back home.
What a lovely garden number 3 has.
Dad must be proud of it.

Oh, Sunflower has got going at once.
And so has the goat.
What super lawnmowers they make!

The chimps can have a rest.
Oh, I think they have dropped off to
sleep in the hot sun.

14

Sunflower has mown the grass.
What's next on the menu?
Oh dear, she's eating Dad's lettuces!

15

No, that's washing, goat, not grass!
Don't eat Dad's pants!

16

Oh dear, here comes Dad.
He is not pleased.
He'll have to get Farmer Gibbon.

Meanwhile those other farmers are
hiding in the bushes.
Can you see them?

Here comes Farmer Gibbon.
He'll soon get those lawnmowers.

19

Oh dear, he's telling Dad about
Bangers and Mash.
I don't think Dad is very pleased.

20

Never mind, it's time to milk the goat.
There, Dad can have a big bucket
of fresh milk.

Oh dear, he's found Bangers and Mash.
Bed! No tea!
It was never like this
on Chimperdale Farm.

Never mind, Mum is creeping up the stairs.
She has two big mugs of fresh milk.
I think those chimps will sleep
after their busy day.

23

Everyone is asleep except Mrs Snitchnose.
She's wondering about her lettuces
and hedge. Don't tell her.
It might get her goat.